BETRAYED

Jeni Burns

Betrayed

Twisted Fate Novella #1

Copyright © 2015

Jeni Burns

c/o Media Jam, LLC

15105-D John J. Delaney Drive; #317

Charlotte, NC 28277

Cover Design By: Valentine Pinova

ISBN: 1-942964-01-3

ISBN-13: 978-1-942964-01-8

ACKNOWLEDGMENTS

There are so many people to thank for their support and guidance along this journey. Each and everyone of them has played a part in the making of this book and to them I am eternally grateful.

First, a special thanks my husband and children for understanding that this is a job and that breakfast food can also be dinner food. Without them, my world is so small and uneventful. They inspire me daily and keep my sense of wonder and adventure alive.

Thank you to all of my amazing writing and critique partners (N.R., D.L., R.P., J.S, S.H., E.R., A.M., D.M.W., T.P., & J.C.). Without you all this book would be so very dull. Reagan Phillips, Denise Leton, and N.R. Ratcliffe all hold a very special place in my squirrelly heart. Also, a huge thank you to all the members of Carolina Romance Writers. This wonderful group of writers is uplifting, supportive, and comforting. Without them, I wouldn't have taken the leap.

A huge thank you to Lara Stokes, Jamie Pejo, and Lauriel Faltin, beta readers extraordinaire. You ladies slay me in all the best ways! Dema is what he is because you made me dig deeper.

Thank you to Valentine Pinova for the amazing cover art. Her patience with my lack of artistic talent is amazing since she could interpret my horribly drawn sketch and create something beautiful.

A huge thank you to everyone who helped edit including, Jan Carol, Help Me Edit Editing Services, and Joshua Strecker. Without these amazingly talented professionals, I'd still be grumbling and muddling through.

And last, but surely not least, thank you to all my friends and family who have stood behind me and cheered me along this journey.

With all my thanks,

~ j

To the woman who always taught me to believe.

To Brenda Taylor with love.

ONE

EARLY 1700's

DELILA DEWSBERRY LIVED a simple life. It didn't mean that it was an unhappy life, but it wasn't a particularly fulfilling one either. As was the custom of the time, Delila had been married before she could slip too far into her teens and be too old for the task, which left her with years of experience in darning, butter churning, and child rearing. Although, these skills didn't give her the satisfaction she had dreamed her life would provide.

Her husband, Thomas, was a reputable man with a well-producing farm and a rotund midsection. Her parents had made the deal with little consideration for her opinion on the matter, but here she was living the life she'd been dealt by Fate, or God, or God-forbid the Goddess.

Delila didn't dare think the word Goddess too often, and she never uttered it aloud. In

1

superstitious times like these, the mere mention of a being other than God would get you stoned, or worse, burned at the stake; and knowing her husband the way she did, Delila knew he would be the first to light the pylon. So Delila kept her beliefs, and her gifts, to herself. Not even Thomas, who slept beside her every night, would guess there was more to her simple life. On solstice nights, she snuck from her bed to perform the spells that kept the land fertile and the livestock well fed. Without her gifts, the farm would have turned into a worthless plot of land long ago.

Soon it would be time to celebrate the date of their betrothal. If Delila had her way, she'd be with child again soon. It did not matter how often she begged for Thomas to take advantage of his marital rites in the last three years, he always balked at the idea. Which is why she had taken to be-spelling him on their anniversary so that she could have one night of passion. Besides, if there was ever a time her husband should want her, she believed the anniversary of their betrothal was it. The need was worth the risk of being discovered a witch.

Their one night of passion was worth the risk of the stockade to combat Delila's loneliness that spanned the other three hundred sixty four nights of the year. It hadn't always taken such lengths to get her husband to notice her, but after stumbling upon Thomas and a farm hand in a passionate embrace, it had become routine for him to turn her away night after night. The allure his lover offered to Thomas had become a constant and growing source of discontent in Delila's life. On more nights that not, she yearned for something more; something greater than her current predicament could offer. Fortunately for her, and Thomas as well she supposed, she developed a new tincture that she believed would finally not only make him amorous, but also produce a child. If all went according to her plan, not only would a child breathe new life into her marriage, but also send Thomas's lover back to wherever he had come from with the outward proof of Thomas and Delila's coupling.

Delila added an extra pinch of powdered oyster to the tincture she ground together and smiled. She had often asked Thomas to convert the extra room out in the barn into a place where she could play with the tools of her father's trade, shaping ordinary things into wearable art, but he always scoffed. To Thomas, a woman's place was in the home caring for her children, not out in some barn whittling hours away on something that men did. So, while he worked, she stole away to the barn and did as she pleased in a makeshift workshop, hopeful that he would never learn of her deception.

With the exception of his infidelity, Thomas was very devout in his beliefs. Beliefs that raised their sons to be God-fearing men and their daughters to be man-serving wives.

Fifteen years into their sham of a marriage, Delila was tired of being a mother to babies, but babies were the only reason Thomas would take her to his side of their marital bed and make her feel whole. The kind of whole she dreamed of being; feminine, purposeful, powerful. To have that she would do what society dictated as conventional. She'd have children and look after a man who loved another; until the man of her dreams came for her, and come for her he would. At least, she hoped he would. This late in her life she often wondered if the mystery man who had wandered through her dreams since childhood, beckoning her to join him, was nothing more than a dream. A dream that promised love, laughter, and excitement. It was those visions that drove her forward, closer to him.

Her destiny.

Her escape.

In the meantime, Delila handed off the day to day routines of childrearing and housework to her eldest daughter, Esther, who was soon of age to be a bride herself. Delila instead, took the time to journal new spells and tinctures including her newest fertility potion. She also found reasons to sneak into the woods surrounding the pastures to spy on Thomas. Something about catching her adulterous husband with the look of love in his eye drove her. To what she still didn't know, but she found herself spending much time comparing herself to the man Thomas so often embraced while she tinkered in her workshop. He, like Thomas, was broad, and when it came to disposition he was abrasive and powerful, even though his station in life made Thomas his superior. Studying them during those intimate times only drove her to desperation; desperation for a lover of her own, one who understood her needs and could fulfill her, making her life all the things it currently was not.

Although it was often said in the company of the womenfolk of the church that keeping secrets from one's spouse opened a door to the devil, Delila didn't believe in such hogwash. It was well known in her family that the devil was just the balancing point for the Goddess.

Without light, dark cannot exist, and the opposite was surely true. Light always shined brightest in a dark room. In the days leading up to her anniversary, Delila often found times to excuse herself from the house, disappearing into the barn. It was there in the solitude she reworked her tincture, a love potion of sorts, and found pleasure at her own hand.

Up until recently, Thomas rarely spoke of the children's existence at all, despite there being twelve of them. Thomas had recently taken to showing their eldest son, Thomas Jr, the ropes around the farm. She would often watch Thomas grooming him to one day take over the responsibility that lay solely on his thick shoulders. But there was never any warmth in it. By day's end both would return to the house weary-eyed and silent. It often made her wonder what it was that Thomas was teaching him.

One day while tinkering in the barn, Delila looked up to find a man standing in the doorway watching her. The appearance of a strange man should've startled her, but her heart raced as excitement coursed through her body. She had known he would come.

Not for a second did she doubt that this was the man from her lifelong visions. Visions that she thought were premonitions of her future husband. Visions she thought had wronged her upon meeting Thomas. Visions that still plagued her on warm summer nights when her lust carried her off into dreams too heated to confess. She could never share these visions with anyone for fear that she'd find herself strung up in an orchard one day, but it didn't keep her from making note when she had them in her journals, and this man was one of her more favored delights.

Unlike Thomas, he was young and hard in the middle, made of muscle and sinew. He stood taller than any man she had ever laid eyes on, and exuded a sense of power. A power she desperately wanted in her life. A power that made her weak in the knees. A power she could claim as her own and not be struck down for possessing.

In her visions he never spoke, yet something about him gave Delila reason to believe his voice would be low, dark, and thick like molasses. The sun behind him played shadows over his face in the peaks and valleys of his sharp features, and even though they had never before spoken, Delila knew him. She knew him body and soul, and she knew his patience would wan quickly if she didn't go to him immediately.

And go to him she did.

Two

A WITCH WITHOUT a broom is no less of a witch, but a witch who couldn't practice her magic felt like less of everything; witch, human, and woman alike. That was the only explanation Delila could give if anyone ever questioned why she did what she did that warm late summer day. Thankfully, Thomas was in the fields, and the barn was empty save her and the man staring at her. The man who exuded power even in the simple way he stood was backlit in the barn doorway, a come hither look etched on his handsome face.

Covered from head to toe in an unseasonable cloak, the stranger was a dark vision. He cocked his head to the side as if he considered making a meal of her, and a chill slithered up Delila's spine at the thought. He was more powerful than she had ever imagined; she felt it in his stare. The idea of having that sort of power at her fingertips, to bend to her will, was intoxicating. Although, she wondered if the power linking her to him was the reason for the heated flush that spread through her body at an impressive speed, or was it the promise of her dreams coming true?

Without a word, he withdrew his hand from beneath the cloak and crooked a long elegant finger at her. Delila's feet acted without her consent as she slowly shuffled toward him. She stopped a mere breath away. His warm spicy breath mingled with hers, dragging her further under whatever spell he wove around them.

He was taller than most of the men she knew, not that it took much to be taller than her, but it still surprised her just how big he was up close. And those shoulders? They were even wider than she remembered from her visions.

Her fingers itched to run over his expansive chest, washboard stomach, and diamond chiseled muscles that she knew lay hidden beneath the cloak. If this was an apparition, Delila wanted every sense available to her so she could create a lasting memory of this very moment.

The stranger laid a warm hand on her cheek and caressed her skin with the pads of his fingers. The smooth skin of his hand stood as a stark contrast to her husband's work-roughened fingers. She could feel his power, the push of his mind against hers, and it startled her. Didn't he know that all he had to do was ask for her willingness? Never before had Delila seen a man as breathtaking as he was, and she wouldn't object to whatever was on his mind. Not after three hundred and some odd days into her year of untouched solitude.

"You needn't do that." She met his dark and stormy gaze. "I can feel it. Your magic is strong." Delila's voice dropped to a whisper. "But I have my own magic." It was liberating to admit it aloud for the first time, even if it was to him; the man who had walked beside her through all of her years, even if only in her dreams. If there was ever someone she could trust with the knowledge of the secrets that she kept so closely guarded, he would be the one. "Are you here for me?"

A spark of something lit his eyes. He nodded.

"Why me?"

He cocked his head to the side and stared her down, but it wasn't enough to make her waver. Delila stood fast, took a deep breath, and waited. She'd already admitted to being a witch and could be burned as such, and now she was about to take a step so brazen that anyone who knew her husband would rush to tell him of her forbidden actions. She grasped at the silky woven cords holding his thick cloak together and gently pulled until the material slipped off his shoulders.

Her breath caught when the fabric slid low enough to reveal taut flesh. Her mystery man's skin was overheated and tanned as if he spent hours in the blistering sun. There wasn't a trace of hair on his chest, nor lower. Delila's eyes took a good long look at what she so often missed, and then something she had never seen before caught her eyes; in addition to the usual appendages hung a long, thickly corded, dark… tail.

Tail? Delila scurried away from him, her heart thundered in her chest a beat that rivaled racing horses, breath froze in her lungs. Delila closed her eyes and rubbed at them with the heels of her hands. She must be mistaken. No man had a tail. Tentatively, she opened first one eye, then the other, to take a better look at the man who was standing closer than she expected.

A playful smirk creased his thin lips as he grasped the unworldly appendage and gave it a long, sure handed stroke. His smile blossomed fuller when he neared the arrowhead shaped end of it, almost as if it gave him pleasure.

"Who... what... are you?" Delila took another step back and was nearly knocked over when from under the rest of the cloak, huge bat-shaped wings covered in thick dark feathers emerged and spread wide.

A hissing sound trickled from his mouth, and dual tips of a forked tongue peeked between his lips. "You have nothing to fear." His voice was low and gravelly. It wrapped around her heart and drew her closer like an invisible rope. "I've been waiting for this moment for a long, long time."

Huge, dark, feather-covered leathery wings beat the air in long strokes, kicking up dust and dirt from the barn floor that pelted her exposed skin until his feet left the ground. "You are here because I granted it to be so. Your dear mother had need of a daughter." He shook his head slowly. "You witches and your daughters.

"The craft does pass nicely between mothers and daughters, but this task was most worthy of the effort." He spoke with a slight slither on the end of his words, but the strange cadence of his voice seduced Delila again one syllable at a time.

"You knew my mother?" Confusion warred with the shock, passion, and desire rolling low in her gut and emerged victorious. "But she's been dead for years."

"Ah, that is true." His wings stopped moving and his bare feet rejoined the dirt floor of the barn. "But it has taken years for you to have your human children and your success in having twelve speaks to your part in fulfilling the prophecy." He dropped his voice an octave and his eyes sauntered over her body. "Besides, I had to see proof that you'd be hearty enough to succeed where others have failed."

"Failed?" Delila stared hard at the sharp angles and lines of his face. He spoke in riddles, almost as if he was the devil himself speaking in tongues.

"Not just any woman is strong enough to carry my child. In fact, there have been hundreds over the years that have tried and failed. But you?" He moved close enough that Delila could feel his breath on her upturned face. "You have successfully brought twelve young into the world, all without losing a single one."

"How do you know about my children?" Nervous energy trilled through her body.

"The prophecies proclaim that the thirteenth child of the heartiest witch in all time shall be able to walk between the worlds. I intend to be that child's father."

Delila swallowed against the lump in her throat and wished that something would begin to make sense. Here she was speaking with a... a what? Surely not an angel if what he was saying was to be believed. So a demon? A demon who was prophesied to father her thirteenth child? That seemed deranged; but when his huge wings enveloped her small frame, the possibilities of what he was became clearer.

"Had I known you were so beautiful, I might have come sooner to enamor you." His fingers slid through her massive locks of hair until he tenderly cradled her head, all while his wings held her in a warm embrace.

"I have waited many centuries for this." He bent his lips to graze hers sending a heated bliss through her body, stealing her breath, yet making her whole. A tentative taste as it were. Pleased with what he found, he turned the next kiss into something Delila had never experienced before. A kiss so deep and passionate it was worthy of melting her bones into a pile of mush.

Her heart pounded in her chest, and every piece of her skin felt overheated and prickly underneath her garments. She reluctantly pried her lips from his, sucking a deep breath of air into her lungs. It did little to calm her, because now there was something inside her that begged for his touch.

A need coursed through Delila's blood that she had yearned for in all her years as Thomas's wife. A need that Thomas had been unable to quench. But she knew that this being before her would drink her in, make her pleasure his mission, and stoke her desire into a burning passion; if only she allowed it.

"Deeeee-lila," her suitor murmured when she ran her hands along the side of his wings. Her name on his tongue was equal parts prayer and summons.

His lips found the sensitive spot beneath her ear that tickled her nerve endings and sent heated sparks through her body. Every moment of his touch against her skin passed with the trumpet of small explosions within. This was what she had been missing her entire life; excitement and power. Things she had always wished for were now within her grasp. Of course, to have them she knew she'd have to pay a price, a price that her mother had warned her would be too much for her soul to bear; but Delila would happily pay it for the chance to find true bliss.

"What is your name?" she whispered. "I need to know your name."

Delila disengaged herself from the cocoon of his wings and stood back. Yet, the longer she gazed at the man before her, the more human he appeared in her mind's eye. Rather than focusing on the tail swinging lazily between his legs, or the wings that he had folded neatly behind his back, Delila was drawn to the rippling muscles and burning desire that lit his eyes on fire. Not to mention, the attention seeking length of what made him all male.

"Demogorgon." The name rumbled from his mouth as if it were a sound instead of a word.

Delila tested the word on her tongue and found herself unable to wrap her mouth around it. Instead, she met his gaze and smiled. "Dema it is."

The smile on his face repaid the humiliation of not being able to utter his name aloud. Dema crooked his finger at her in silent command, and the twist of his lips fell back into a hard, straight line. Like the good little wife that she was trained to be, Delila obeyed. Without ceremony, Dema flicked a hand toward the heavy barn door and it swung into place before her eyes. A second wave of his hand had the massive bar, which acted as a lock, secured in place.

Unlike the manual labor Dema accomplished with the simple use of magic, it seemed that undressing her was something he took great pains to do by his own hand. Fabric slid slowly down her body as cool air prickled her sensitive skin only to be soothed by the unusually heated touch of his bare hands. When she finally stood before him as naked and exposed as he, Delila didn't feel the all-too familiar urge to cover her exposed flesh. Instead, a feeling of empowerment washed over her in a flare of bravado. Unlike Thomas, who preferred her under the cover of darkness, Dema looked his fill, his pupils rounding into dark orbs while his fingers twitched at his side like petulant children needing to touch what they've been told to let alone.

When it seemed he could restrain himself no more, Dema took the single step required to press his body against hers. The heat of his body shocked her bared flesh, but Delila welcomed every bit of him that he offered.

Within seconds they became a tangle of limbs on a bed of straw. Each second whirled past in a blur while her body struggled to stay in the present moment, relishing the memory of every touch, kiss, and caress. These memories would fuel the rest of her days.

As Dema moved over her, the roughness of the straw chafed her delicate skin. His hardness pressed onto her softness only adding to the friction at her back. His mouth tasted her with his skilled tongue lapping and licking across her chest. When it slipped lower into her womanly folds and found the apex of her sex, she caught her breath and shuddered. What was this ministration he practiced? Time stood still as her brain rushed to make sense of the sensations he caused. Never before had a man's tongue been near this part her body. May the Goddess forgive her, but if there was one thing she could take from Dema's lovemaking, it would be this.

Unable to pull her thoughts from the sensations that threatened to overwhelm her, Delila closed her eyes and allowed the feelings to take over. Flames licked at her from the inside out until her body felt moments away from going up in an inferno. His tongue slicked across her most sensitive juncture until it slipped within the confines of her body.

Licking, sucking, tugging, each gentle nibble of teeth sent a spasm of ecstasy rolling through her body. The sexual God between her legs purred in satisfaction. Aftershocks rocked her over-sensitized body until the cool air of his departure brought her back to reality. As she sat up, she scoured the barn for any indicator of where her mystery lover had gone, but the only thing that remained was the dark cloak he had worn abandoned where it had fallen in the dirt.

Delila's heart sank. She closed her eyes and tried to conjure Dema back into being with the power of her mind, but when she opened them the barn was as empty as it had been moments before. If not for the heated hum of the flesh between her thighs as proof of her dalliance, she might be easily convinced it had been a dream.

Delila dressed without any fanfare and was surprised to find the barn door unbarred and slightly ajar. Was it her lover's doing? The thought gave her hope. With a smile on her face, and a happy tune in her head, she went about the rest of her day.

*****

The next day, as soon as the children were settled for the day, and Thomas and her eldest sons had left for a trip into town, Delila raced to the barn. As she burst over the threshold, she was pleased to find Dema leaning against an empty stable door exposed and aroused. The moment she stepped further into the barn the door swung shut behind her and the thud of the pine stud falling into place spurred her forward movement.

Dema wrapped his arms around her body and took possession of her lips, all without speaking. It was as if he had known she would be here looking for him again this day. He lifted her into his arms and twirled her, moving them steadily toward the rear wall of the unoccupied stall. With a nod of his head, Dema opened the door that led to the far pasture away from the view of the house so that sunlight bathed the stall with warm light. The smile Delila had grown to anticipate slithered across Dema's face as he went to work disposing of her clothes.

Her pulse raced when he lifted her higher into the air and pinned her to the cool wooden wall of the stall so that her back was met by the cold wood, and her front was heated by the heady combination of sunlight and Dema. He nudged her legs around his waist and carefully lowered her onto his waiting prick.

A soft gasp escaped her lips as the fullness of him pushed into the most private parts of her. He took his time rocking his hips against her hungry body, reaching places inside of her that had never been exposed to such sensations. Dema nibbled at her neck, a tantalizing combination of his sweeping tongue and blunt teeth scrapping her skin.

Delila lost herself in the feel of him and barely noticed when he shifted until he was standing upright and her body was unsupported on his. Arms of steel tucked her tightly against his chest with just enough care to hold her close but not hurt her.

Step after step, he moved them out of the barn and into the sunlight until she could feel the heat of the sun on her bare back matching the heat of Dema on her front. Every movement he made slipped her further down his cock and sent a jolt of passion straight to the core of her. The unfurling of his wings took her by surprise, but it was quickly surpassed by the feel of the wind against her superheated skin as they took to the sky.

There was nothing in Delila's life that could ever be compared to this. Flying through the air in an intimate embrace was more than her mind could comprehend, that was until his tail went to work stroking, teasing, probing. The appendage smacked across her rear in rapid succession, coaxing a long moan of desire from her throat. Dema took the opportunity to fill the space between her lips with his hot tongue, and that wicked tail of his snaked it's way into a private place where Delila had never been touched before. He filled her body so fully, she was afraid she'd split in two.

The beating of his wings pulsed through every inch of his body and echoed into hers with a rhythm faster than a prized racehorse. Wrapped in his protective embrace they twisted through the air, high above the prying eyes of anyone below. As they rose above the thin layer of clouds, Delila struggled to catch enough air to fill her fear frozen lungs. Inch by delicious inch Dema's prick snaked deeper and deeper into her body until it seemed he owned every part of her being, with the empty shell of the woman she had been before him the only thing that remained.

Thrust after thrust, caress after caress, the joy of his touch slowly rebuilt her into a new woman until the sensations were too much. Her eyes sealed shut against the explosion that wracked her body. If yesterday's tryst had shocked the foundation of her world, then today's destroyed it, leaving her world a blaze of fire and ash. Aftershocks took over her body's ability to make sense of her surroundings.

Dema trailed a pathway of kisses down her neck to the hollow of her throat. "Again my goddess. I need you again," he panted against her skin.

Inside her, Delila could feel the swell of his prick and tail as they renewed their vigorous demands deep within her flesh. Her body hummed and reveled at his insistence, while her mind fought to capture every moment of this bliss in detail. She clung to his corded neck, her hands holding fast to the taut muscles beneath his skin while his hands went to work on her breasts, toying with her sensitive nipples. Dema took every opportunity to twist, bank, and dive through the air as she reached new heights of ecstasy. When she worried that she'd fall, he planted a firm hand on her back and dove deep.

Deep into her.

Deep toward the ground.

The fear of death combined with the thrill of the moment was enough to send her traitorous body into a bliss that bordered on oblivion. A howl more animal than human tickled her ears as Dema pulsed inside her. Air rushed at them. Her eyes flew open only to find the ground drawing nearer and nearer.

"Dema!" Her scream was lost in the wind as she struggled against him.

She clawed at his chest while panic held her hostage, frozen in his ironclad grip. One final twitch of his prick and his wings opened wide, slowing their descent.

"Ah, you are wicked my witch, not a goddess at all." The smile on his face dripped with innuendo. "I had planned to woo you much longer, but your body is more greedy than I had imagined." She felt his tail withdraw from between her cheeks and then a quick snap stung the round globes. "You are an elixir that I could become addicted to." His words tickled her heart and sent it soaring. Dema changed their course until the far pasture came into sight.

Unlike their fast, furious, flying mating, their landing was soft and gentle. He lifted her from his still hard prick, carried her into the empty stall, and laid her on a bed of fresh hay where he took his time cleansing her with that devilish tongue. It reawakened Delila's weary body until she sparked to life like grease dancing in a hot pan.

One more tryst couldn't hurt, could it?

With a grin on her face that she feared matched his wicked one, Delila took him in her mouth; an action that gave him more reasons to howl. If there was a way to put this moment, these feelings, and the joy she felt in a bottle for safe keeping she would, but for now she would have to live with enjoying every illicit moment. And she did, under the protection of a hastily woven spell, until the sun began to sink low in the sky and she could no longer ignore the demands of her regular life.

Three

BY THE END of the day Delila's stomach roiled and cramped. Her dinner refused to stay put, and she would swear that she could feel the familiar flutter of life deep within her womb. It was preposterous that one encounter with a strange man would leave her feeling this way. Perhaps it was guilt that plagued her, rather than the idea that what surely had been an encounter with a powerful being had resulted in her being with child so soon.

The children dutifully went about their routines without so much as a sideways glance at her, although Delila couldn't lose the feeling of being watched. Thomas was his usual apathetic self. He sat in silence throughout supper, only moving to give cursory pats to each child's head on his way to bed at the end of the meal.

That night, Delila found herself in her usual spot beside a snoring Thomas, and wished she were elsewhere. Like most every night, she laid beside a man who would be just as content if she didn't exist as he would with her at his side. Now that she had experienced how it could be with a man who desired her, when the loneliness crept into her soul and beat at her heart until the tears she kept carefully dammed inside began to spill, it shattered what little hold she had on the cyclone of emotions coursing through her body. They streamed down her face as the sting of his constant rejection grew hard in her chest. She needed an escape, an escape to anywhere other than here beside Thomas.

It wasn't the first time during her marriage that she had snuck from her marital bed in an attempt to escape the resentment and rejection that swirled like an angry cyclone in her soul. If her life continued down this path of dejection and hurt, it wouldn't be the last either.

However, this time as Delila slid into the night she found herself headed to the barn. She lit a lantern and hung it on a peg in the stall from earlier in the day. She plucked Dema's cape from the cubby in her workshop where she had hidden it the previous day and held it to her chest, inhaling his smoky scent deep into her lungs. She wrapped it around her shoulders and went in search of a blanket. Never before tonight had the barn held so much appeal to her, but the memories of Dema combined with the smell of him wrapped around her body only added to the appeal. Appeal that increased when the unshakeable feeling of being watched became less visceral and more weighted.

"Deeeee-lila." Her lover was back, but this time his voice wasn't slow and seductive; it was comforting, warm, and soft. Dema knelt bare beside her and traced gentle fingers over the tracks of dried tears on her face. He followed with gentle kisses and soft strokes until her skin flushed and desire sparked to life. "I can be his undoing. All you must do is ask."

His offer whispered the barest threat of honesty in her ears. She smiled and sunk into his embrace, feeling tender and loved, safe and warm. This was where she belonged; in the loving care of a man who cherished her instead of one who ignored her and deemed her irrelevant except for maintaining the appearance of decency.

"I refuse to let him hurt you again, witch. He will pay for such actions with his life."

"He doesn't mean it, Dema." Delila lowered her lashes and hoped the lie she so often told herself would settle in him the way it had in her soul. "Not loving me isn't a sin he should be punished for."

"Nonsense. I saw what he did, ignoring you and leaving you to do all that is required to maintain that brood of his children. It was unwarranted even by my standards, and *I* torture souls for fun."

Her breath caught in her throat as she dared meet his eyes. The wings, the tail, the forked tongue; he was a demon and she would do well to remember it, because if Dema was what she thought he was, the pleasure he offered wasn't free.

"What did you think I was? I know you didn't mistake me for an angel, but how could you not see me as the devil that I am?"

"The devil?" She tripped over her words and quickly withdrew her hands from his body. Delila knew Dema wasn't like anyone she had ever met, but surely he was exaggerating. Wasn't he?

"Darling, that you know my name is an honor not many achieve." He traced a finger down her sternum and circled it around her navel. "That you can endure mating with me without your veins turning black from poisoning is proof enough to me that you are the witch destined to bring my rule onto this plane. If we can bring a daughter into this world, she will open the Overworld to me."

"The Overworld?" Delila froze as his fingers delved into the soft flesh between her legs.

"Mortals call it heaven, but I can tell you from experience it is nothing like the heaven I found within you." Hunger danced in his eyes, swelling dark and mysterious.

The forked tip of his tongue flicked at his lips, lips that pressed against her navel in a delicate kiss. The hard length of him arched into her and the thrum of his fingers played her like an instrument until she was floating on a wave of passion. When she feared she could stand no more of his skilled ministrations, he finally claimed her as his own, but this time wasn't full of high-flying passionate demands. Tender, soothing strokes mingled with whispered promises that dominated the loving until her body reached climax. The stars before her eyes shone brighter than the ones in the sky that night.

"You are the most beautiful of my conquests, witch." Dema laid behind her and wrapped her still quaking body in his arms. His wings folded around them holding the warmth against her skin. "You constantly surprise me, my love." He laid a hand on her stomach and sighed. "It's already begun."

Fatigue and satisfaction dragged her beneath

the canopy of sleep as his words twisted into streams of dreams.

*****

Feather-light kisses and the warm glow of the new day, roused Delila from her slumber.

Dema's words tickled her ear. "I wish you'd permit me to finish him."

"I can't allow that. My soul would be forever ruined." The excuse was trite, but it was the best she could devise.

"Your soul? Now you choose to worry about its purity? You've broken your marriage vows. You've conferred with the devil, and you're carrying his seed in your womb right now. But the idea of disposing of your husband causes you concern?" He shook his head and unraveled himself from their entanglement. "I will spare him for now, but know this; you are mine. I will not share you with that wretched being." His dark eyes pierced straight through to her heart. "I own your needs, your desires, your wanting, all of which there will be many. You must promise me that you will not allow him to take them from me."

Her stomach clenched and her mouth went dry as the panic of giving up appearances washed over her. For too long, she had done whatever was required to keep herself safe from the prying eyes of those who would condemn her a witch and kill her as such.

"I cannot stop him if he desires to take his marital rites," she whispered, eyes downcast. It wasn't that Thomas would want to take such liberties, but if Dema was right and she was already with child, she would face worse than endless imprisonment, or Goddess-forbid banishment, for a proven pregnancy outside of her marriage, especially if the father was proven to be the devil himself. That revelation would carry the penalty of death; and a painful death at that. She would need Thomas to help create the illusion of a happy marriage; he owed her that much considering she did the same for him.

Dema tugged her chin up until their eyes met. "You have the power to refuse him. I can feel it. You must choose to use it."

Delila offered no further rebuttal. Instead, she gave a slight nod. Dema didn't need to know that she would sleep with Thomas to save her life. Albeit a life that would be deemed worthless given her transgression with the devil. A seductive smile warmed his face.

The sound of Thomas approaching the barn reached her ears a moment before the protest of the wooden doors sounded. Panic flooded her system. With eyes wide, she turned to Dema only for him to fling his cloak over his body and burst through the stall door into the far pasture.

"What was that?" Thomas yelled and retreated from the barn long enough for her to redress in her nightclothes. When Thomas returned, his face twisted in confusion upon finding Delila exiting the stall. "What are you doing out here in your nightclothes? Have you lost your mind, woman?"

She lowered her eyes. It was best not to engage him; from past experiences she knew that left bruises, but it was so tempting to let him see the flush that still stained her cheeks.

"I awoke early and thought I saw something creeping into the barn," she lied. "I thought it best to let you sleep." She shuffled her feet toward the door, but Thomas blocked her path.

He reached out a meaty hand, snaked his fingers around her upper arm, and squeezed. "Wife, I know you prefer your workshop to the duties of your station, but appearances must be kept."

"I need to go start breakfast, Thomas." He added enough pressure to her arm that her muscles ached beneath her skin and she cringed in pain. "Please, Thomas."

"Keep in mind the time, Delila. The workers will be coming soon, and you shouldn't be found out here in your bedclothes."

Delila nodded until his hand released her, then she quickly left him alone in her place of sanctuary.

FOUR

NIGHT AFTER NIGHT, as the summer faded into autumn, Delila and Dema escaped into each other; fueled by passion and fire. Her body swelled with child, but much faster than ever before. She took precautions to dress in larger garments that hid the evidence of her transgressions, but with the rapid rate of her growing midsection, she would soon need Thomas to take his joy in her body.

Dema languished over the swelling of Delila's body, taking careful and gentle strokes inside of her until it drove her mad. One autumn day as Delila stood bare before him, sunlight warming her skin through the open stable door, Dema brushed sensual strokes of his tongue over her sun kissed skin.

"Witch, you take my breath away. Who would have known that I could be so enchanted by a mere human?" He kissed a circle around her protruding navel then laid his head on the mound of flesh. "I can hear him," he whispered. "Tell me how it feels to know a life we created is growing inside of you?"

"It's unlike anything I've ever experienced. It's growing much faster than any of my other children did." She slid her hands over her rounded stomach. "Are you sure it's a boy?"

Dema nodded. "He will be a great force in the world. One that will tear down the boundaries between the worlds and walk between them."

Hours later, when their desire had been sated, they drifted off into the sleep that comes from pure bliss.

In the early morning hours, Delila felt guilt rise in her chest. The regret as she crept from her bed of hay and blankets to skulk back into her home made the stark reality of her traitorous ways burden her soul. There was no question that she loved Dema, loved him as she could never love Thomas, but that love was undoing her; unraveling her carefully constructed facade, leaving her defenseless against whatever this baby might bring.

Nervous energy drove her momentum for the day. The act of scrubbing floorboards, hanging laundry, and polishing silver were mere distractions, but it was the best she could do given the circumstances. While she paced the floor of her kitchen, Dema popped into the room with all the grace a fallen angel possessed.

"What's kept you from me today, my witch?" His voice low and dark started the slow burn in the pit of her stomach. Dema stood statue still undressing her with his eyes. "I thought we had a standing date." He cocked his head to the side. "Or have you grown tired of me?"

The familiar sizzle of heat rushed through her

body, bringing her fully to life. "I've been waiting for Thomas."

"What does he have to do with us?" His already dark eyes turned to pitch and for the first time Delila feared the demon before her.

"I'm beginning to show." As far as explanations for hiding from her lover went, it wasn't much. It was the best she could come up with when faced with the sheer displeasure rolling off Dema in waves and the menacing stare that pinned her to the spot.

"And what does that have to do with us?" Venom clung to his every syllable, dark, menacing, poisonous. It chilled her to her very core.

"Everything. If he can't claim this child as his own, I have no future."

"I can have him dealt with. If he was no longer here to claim it no one would know that he wasn't the child's father."

"I cannot let you do that. Thomas is innocent in all this."

"Innocent? He treats you like a slave. He goes about his life pretending that you are one of his wards, a responsibility that he must endure. There is no love or loyalty there."

"Promise me that you will let him alone." She could not allow Dema to take Thomas's life for her own selfish desires, even if doing so would mean she would be free to live her life as she deemed fit. This was a decision that only she could make, and her soul wasn't up to bearing the weight of one more sin.

As if to echo her thoughts, the proof of her infidelity tumbled in her womb. She wrapped her hands around the bump in her midsection and met her lover's eyes. "Under no circumstances will you harm Thomas. For the sake of our child, you will let him be."

Her demand rolled off his broad shoulders with a shrug.

"Witch, I think you forget who is the more powerful being here."

Delila flinched, expecting malice, but humor was Dema's weapon of choice.

"Keep in mind our conversation. Your pleasure is mine, you promised it to me. So do what you must. I'll be here waiting to offer you my services after you finish with him, and I promise your body will sing like the goddess you are." His brows wiggled to drive his promise home.

Delila's heart leapt, as did his manhood, at the unsaid promise hanging in the air between them. Now all she had to do was find a way to kill two birds with the one stone that would keep them all alive.

FIVE

NIGHT FELL ON the sleepy farm, and Demogorgon waited hidden in the darkness. It wasn't in his nature to distrust, despite the human rumors to the contrary, but this day made him rethink his stance.

Delila's actions today had given him pause. In the few months they had spent together he had become enamored with her openness and genuine nature. In fact, he never considered she would betray him; until today. When she had avoided the barn, he had gone in search of her. For a while he had watched over her in silence, unseen through the cloak he wore. Something was definitely wrong with his lover. While Delila typically puttered about with her metal designs, today she was satisfied with the mundane tasks of her housewife station. Secretly watching her had become a habit ever since their first mating. She was a drug he would never tire of taking, a heaven that he could experience on Earth.

But there was something weighing on her

today, that much he could divine from her actions. It caused him physical pain to restrain himself from using his magic to pull the information straight from her brain, but confronting her had yielded little fruit in the information gathering department. Instead, the endeavor left him unsettled with a nagging sense of dread.

Demogorgon returned to the realm of shadows that hid him from human view. After all the children had been tucked into their respective beds, he followed his love into the room she shared with her husband. The idea of Delila being so close to another man, when Demogorgon himself wanted her, was enough to kick off his anger. As she sprinkled a powdered substance into a cup of liquid at the bedside, and shrugged out of her nightgown, it was rage that took hold of him.

Stunned into silence, Demogorgon withdrew further into the shadows and watched. Thomas walked past his bared wife unseeing. The man sat on the bed's edge and downed the contents of the tainted glass. Demogorgon waited as the seconds ticked into minutes. Thomas then sank into the bed beside his wife with less than a glance in her direction, until Delila pressed herself against his side and began stroking the length of him through his night garments.

What in all the world was she thinking? This was his woman, yet here she was throwing herself at a man who wouldn't see her if she burst into flames. Why would she choose to spend her night being rejected by her husband before coming to him? It made no sense. What made it worse was that her husband, a man that Demogorgon knew preferred the company of other men, became aroused as if he was bespelled. Bespelled. The tincture? The man's arousal? Everything clicked into place. His beloved was spelling her husband. But to what end? All his beloved needed do was sedate her husband and use her gift to plant a memory in the man's mind that would convince him of his part in the conception of the child growing within her.

Before Demogorgon could contemplate it further, Delila kissed her husband and threw a leg over Thomas's mid-section. Demogorgon stared, transfixed by the beauty of her body, as she took her pleasure from the man beneath her. With every thrust, grunt, and moan he lost a piece of his heart.

How dare she do this to him? To them? Pain that only rivaled his falling from Heaven exploded in Demogorgon's chest and whipped through his body on a searing wave of fiery torment. A howl ripped from his core unfiltered and animalistic.

Broken.

Delila stopped mid-claim and whipped her head around toward him. Her eyes went round. The deer faced with the wolf.

Beneath her, Thomas shuddered, arched off the bed, and groaned, but Delila didn't look away. Instead she shrank into herself and fell away from the robust man. She wrapped herself in a thin layer of cloth and slid from the bed.

Demogorgon stalked from the room with little care for keeping his presence a secret any longer. If the witch had seen him his cloak was fading. What was to be expected when his emotions ran so tight and close to the surface like this? He paced the floorboards of her home and debated tearing the house apart board by board, but the thought of hurting Delila sent a chill through him.

Comprehension flooded through his body. He had misread her. He had fallen for her eagerness, and what started out as a means to an end had evolved into something more. Something Demogorgon had come to cherish. And seeing her with that man? It shattered his resolve. Delila had played a game with him, just as he had done with her. A small hand wrapped around his arm.

"Dema," Delila's voice shook as she held tight to him. "I thought I told you I'd meet you in the barn?" Her whispered question ignited his fury further. Was she still trying to hide him from her husband's knowledge? Demogorgon could hear Thomas coughing in the bedroom and wondered if this would be the moment where she would finally be forced to choose.

"I have no words for you, witch." He glared at her and tried to read the look on her face. "You dare lie with that man after what we've started?" Accusation mixed with hurt. His words sounded foreign to his own ears.

"Please, give me a minute to explain." She fiddled with the sheet wrapped around her.

"No." He wanted to turn and walk away, but the well of tears pooling in her eyes gave him pause. Despite her damned betrayal, his heart still yearned for her. Her tenderness and warmth. Her acceptance and love.

"I needed him to believe the baby could be his," she whispered. "If I didn't do this now, he would never have believed me. I did this for us. For you." Her voice cracked on a sob. "He means nothing to me, and I am nothing to him."

She slid to the ground her face upturned. "I can prove it to you, let me show you." Her husband calling her name through a fit of coughs cut her words short.

Turning from her, Demogorgon caught sight of Thomas as he staggered through the doorway. His face was swollen, breath ragged, and his gait listed to the left. But it was what Demogorgon saw that the witch could not that made the world right again. Thomas's soul was pulling away from his earthly body.

"Thomas? What's wrong?" Delila asked.

Demogorgon stepped aside as his witch went to her husband. In moments, it was clear to him. Thomas had been poisoned. Demogorgon watched as darkness streaked through the man's veins. Somehow, the fallen's curse had touched the human. Touched him and now would condemn the man's soul to the Underworld where he would be at Demogorgon's mercy. Laughter spread through him. What a twist of fate.

"What's wrong with you? You must help me heal him," his witch called.

But it was too late. The man's soul had spilt from his body and there was little Demogorgon would be able to do to repair it. Besides, the only thing that cured the Curse was tears, not just any tears, but ones of the fallen. He watched as the soul twisted and turned in the air, confused by the appearance of his mortal body at his feet and the

Devil by his side.

"What has happened? Why is my wife crying?"

"She's weeping for you, the dearly departed." Demogorgon answered wordlessly. *"She will blame herself for your untimely death,"* he added.

"But why?" The shape of the soul began to shimmer, losing the delicate foothold it had on this plane.

"Because, she believes she has poisoned you."

"Never."

"But she did." Demogorgon raised his brow at the soul before him. *"She poisoned your marriage with betrayal and your body with the proof of it. My seed grows inside her."*

"Dema, please you must help him." Delila's cries flowed freely now.

"She speaks your name," the soul gasped.

"That she does," Demogorgon agreed.

"But how?"

"I'm the poison in your marriage. Her body belongs to me."

The witch rose to her feet and launched herself into his arms. "Please, lover. Don't make me suffer for what I had to do. Help me. Bring him back to me. I promise I will never lie with him again so long as he is alive."

"Witch, I cannot undo what's been done. And if

I could? I still would not." It was heartless, Demogorgon knew, but he cared not even the slightest. This was best for them. With her husband gone, Delila would be his for the rest of time and together they would rule this plane, and the rest, as the prophecy had promised.

Delila stepped out of his embrace and slapped his face; the sting danced along his skin. "You choose to punish me." Accusation hung thick in the air between them.

"I choose to do my job." Plain and simple.

Delila took another step away from Demogorgon, raised her arms, and began to chant.

Her words struck him with a force greater than any blow had ever landed, and at his feet he felt the pull of the Underworld. No. She couldn't have the power to send him back. Could she? Before he could fully comprehend the situation, Demogorgon was being yanked back into Hell. It was only in his last moments on Earth that he thought to grab Thomas's soul and drag it down with him.

Six

Five Years Later

DELILA STOOD AT the kitchen window and watched her oldest sons come in from the fields. In the years since Thomas had passed they had done wonders keeping up the farm. Esther, her daughter, had married a young gentleman in town, and his family had offered a substantial dowry for her hand which had repaid the debts the farm had incurred until her sons were old enough to work it on their own. Her next youngest daughters, Rosie and Patricia, were also newly married, both with young children.

Her sons however, remained unmarried and stayed home tending the farm. Their finances were in ruin from overpaying the workers in the aftermath of Thomas's death, but her sons worked hard to look after her and support the younger children so that she could go about her day as she always had. She did her part by saving the little money they made for the bare essentials and occasional treats.

Even surrounded as she was by her family, Delila's nights were lonely, and her bed was cold. On those nights, she missed the comfort she had once found in Dema's arms; but still to this day, she couldn't forgive him.

Had he ever really understood her he would have saved Thomas. It would have saved her the scrutiny of the townsfolk, especially when her thirteenth child came into the world shortly after Thomas's passing looking nothing like either of them.

Delila's unruly blond curls had made their way through the majority of their twelve children, and when they didn't, it was still Thomas's pale straight locks that took root. But where her other children were fair, Drammelech was dark. Where their eyes were shades of blue, his reminded her of the darkness at midnight. Where they were typical human children in all aspects, he was something other.

Elech, as she took to calling him, looked as human as his siblings, but he grew faster than any of them ever had. He appeared almost as old as Fredrick, who was just on the cusp of turning ten, despite the fact that Elech was barely over four years.

Elech worried her. Delila noticed the looks that he got in town. The adults gave him sideways glances, the children stopped and stared; but the girls? The girls followed behind and whispered sweet nothings. At such an early age, he was already developing into the spitting image of his father minus the wings, tail, and tongue. Delila couldn't be sure how it was that she had managed to have a human looking child, but she was grateful it was what had come to pass.

Today, Elech accompanied his oldest brothers in from the farm. Although she had insisted that he remain home with the rest of the younger children, Elech had somehow convinced Tommy, her eldest, that he was indeed the best farm hand available. And based on the wide smile decorating Tommy's face, Elech hadn't been exaggerating.

Her five oldest boys all stopped to wipe their feet and leaned down to kiss her cheek as they entered the house. It had become a tradition after Thomas had passed, one that she cherished. Elech followed, placing a gentle kiss on her hand as he entered.

"How was it today?" she asked.

"Elech helped mend the fence in the far pasture," Tommy beamed. "It was like he was born for farm work." He ruffled his younger brothers dark locks. "Tomorrow we will move the stock into that pasture and prepare the field for plowing."

"Very good, Tommy. Your father would be so proud of you."

Her oldest ducked his head as a splash of red colored his cheeks. He was a humble boy and, much as she hated to admit it, would soon leave her to start a family of his own.

*****

After dinner, Delila found herself at the kitchen window staring at the barn in the sinking sunlight.

"Mother, why do you always look so sad?"

She hadn't heard Elech approach. He placed a hand on her elbow and she turned to meet his questioning eyes.

"I'm not sad, darling. I'm just remembering a different time. One from long ago." It was the truth, or at the very least, the best version of the truth she could muster.

"Mother, can you tell me again about father?"

It was a question that often graced his lips. And every time she answered it a tiny piece of her heart fell away. Delila began to retell her well-practiced tale of Thomas as she recounted stories from the lives of Elech's siblings. Stories full of love and compassion. Stories that the other children would never remember because they weren't full of truth. But this evening Elech stopped her before she sank into the familiar twisted tales.

"I've asked you this many times," he paused as if searching for the words. "But this time can you tell me about my real father?"

The words washed over her, cool, even, and sure. At not quite five he knew the truth. Impossible.

"Elech, I'm not sure I understand. Thomas was your father. I've told you that."

"Then why does the man in the dark cloak keep coming to me?"

Her heart skipped a beat. It wasn't true. It couldn't be true. There was no way that Dema was able to once again walk between the planes. She had banished him to the Underworld. If the ancient texts passed down from generation to generation of witches were to be believed, his banishment would be permanent unless someone with power called him back to the surface.

Good Goddess, please let there not be someone skilled enough to call him forth.

In her panic Delila had forgotten Elech.

"Mother?"

"Tell me everything, Elech. Who is this man, and what has he said to you?" She lowered herself to the floor, knelt before her son, and met his eyes.

"Mother, you're scaring me."

"I'm sorry my son, but you must tell me everything. I cannot protect you unless you tell me." Her heart thumped against her ribs as if it were about to break free.

"He's always been there Mother. But now that I help Tommy, I see him more. He walks with me in the pastures and keeps watch while I work." Elech twisted his hands in his lap as he told his story.

"He never speaks to me, not really, but today I asked him his name and he told me to call him 'Father.' I told him I had a father, and that he was dead, but the man told me that I was mistaken." Elech turned his dark eyes on her and waited for her response.

Thoughts flooded Delila from every corner of her mind. They paraded through like a stampede of angry animals out for blood. Her breathing matched the erratic beat of her heart while her mind flailed.

And then the world stopped.

Darkness.

Nothingness.

Silence.

Delila opened her eyes and found herself wrapped in the security of dark, warm wings. She must be dreaming, and if it went like the other dreams of her winged lover, this one would carry her off into ecstasy. Dema opened his mouth and unfamiliar words fell from his lips. Her head throbbed with pain, and the smell of copper hung close to her nose. Had she fallen? She couldn't remember. Her vision clouded again and the pounding in her head lessened.

"I'm here, witch. I will see to it that you are healed."

"Healed?" His words bounced around in her empty head while she wrestled with the realization that her heart rested still against her ribs.

"My lovely witch. It isn't your time yet. You need to raise our son and give him what he needs to fulfill his destiny."

"Dema? Is that really you?" Confusion warred with her desire to close her eyes and rest.

"Do you trust me, little witch?"

"I dare not trust my heart to you again." Her words tumbled on top of one another until they formed nothing more coherent than a jumble of sounds.

"Lie here and close your eyes." His voice was as thick as the darkness surrounding her, yet it kept the monsters lurking in the shadows at bay. She couldn't see them, but she could sense them. Feel them hunting her; watching and waiting, much like Dema had done, but their hunger far surpassed even his insatiable appetite.

The flutter of her lashes gave way and Delila witnessed the most beautiful thing she had ever seen. Crouched over her was Dema, head bowed over her chest, his wings shielded her body from what hid in the shadows. Tears streamed from his eyes. This was the angel she knew. Fallen or not, this sealed in her mind his place in the world. One by one the tears fell to her chest and warmth seeped inside and spread throughout every inch of her. A flicker started in her chest and slowly became a rhythmic pulse. Breath filled her lungs, and Delila relished the feel of it. Tired, she closed her eyes.

When she felt herself again the sound of quiet sobbing pulled her back to reality. She struggled to her knees. Elech's tear-streaked face was inches away from her as he rocked back and forth. Huddled behind him in the corner of the room was the man she had once hoped to never see again.

Seeing them in the same room was like looking at one of them through the looking glass of time. Elech was a younger version of Dema, and Dema was a seasoned, larger-than-life version of her son. Both sat on the floor, arms wrapped around their legs, heads bowed. Identical locks of charcoal hair fell over identical foreheads solidifying the comparisons she often drew in her mind. Neither seemed to be aware of the other, but Delila could feel their identical anguish, regret, and loss.

Without thought she crawled to her son and enveloped him in her arms. Words were too much, but the simple feel of him against her was enough. From the corner of her eye she caught the moment that realization collided with her angel lover.

Dema's legs wobbled as he rose to his feet and walked the short distance to where Delila sat holding their son. His wings dragged behind him, worn, and molting. He laid one hand on her head, and one on Elech's, but said nothing. Delila searched his eyes for something, anything, that would reveal his thoughts, but sadness was all she found. He simply nodded at her and with what appeared to be great effort he disappeared into thin air.

$Seven$

DELILA WENT THROUGH days, weeks, months, years before she laid eyes on Dema again. Elech no longer mentioned him, and she had finally stopped looking for him when he next appeared. It was a rainy day; the type that carried a whiff of the cold to come. While the boys headed out to tend the field, Delila sat by the fire with the girls, working through the darning.

It was well past midday when the sound of gunfire echoed through the house. It wasn't unusual for such a sound, what with the predators that stalked the farm, but it still sent a shiver down Delila's spine. Another shot rang out and a howl followed.

A human howl.

Delila bolted upright and ran through the house. She burst through the back door in time to see Edward and Joseph half carrying, half dragging, Tommy between them.

"What happened?" She gathered her skirt in hand and ran toward her sons.

"A wolf," Edward gasped.

"Elech tried to scare it off, but he missed," Joseph added.

"Elech?" Puzzled she looked around for her youngest son.

"Fredrick is with him," Tommy mumbled, his face ashen. He slumped to the ground.

With dread lodged firmly in a tight ball deep in her stomach, Delila knelt beside him, and took a closer look at the gaping wound that oozed on his side. A tentative touch around the area sent her son into body quaking tremors. Rain fell from the skies, mixed with the blood, and washed it down his body.

Her rain-slicked hair clung to her face, obscuring everything but Tommy from her view. It was the death of Thomas all over again. Here she sat, watching one of the men in her life struggling for every breath while all she could do was hold his hand and cry.

Delila threw her head back as a sob ripped from her chest. The heavens hung above her, close enough to touch through the low-laying clouds, yet far enough that she clung to this moment. This moment where she could still hold her son in her arms, one last memory she could hold onto for the rest of her years.

A hand perched on her shoulder; firm yet gentle. "It's time, witch."

She turned her eyes to her fallen angel. Of course he was here. He was wrapped in his cloak and time stood frozen as he spoke.

"Not yet," she begged.

"It's time."

Dema's eyes were darker and his skin paler than usual. Had he been human she would've thought him ill.

"You need to let me take him now," Dema insisted. "If not me, then one of my minions will come for him, and they won't care for him as I will."

"You cannot condemn my son to the Underworld," she cried. "What has he done to deserve such a sentence?"

"It's not for me to decide who goes where. It's a choice predetermined before life."

"No," she moaned. "Not him too."

"It will be a part of the journey his soul requires to reach it's full potential in the spiritual realm one day." He gave her shoulder a gentle squeeze.

Delila watched as Dema nodded to someone she could not see and offered his hand. Tears fell heavy, pregnant with her sorrow. She followed him with her eyes, hoping that for just the briefest of moments, she could see the soul of her eldest son, but in the blink of her eye Dema was gone. She turned back to Tommy's body and found it empty. His blood no longer flowed. His chest no longer rose. His heart no longer beat.

"Mother, I'm so sorry." She looked up, surprised to see Elech standing over her. He seemed bigger now, somehow changed forever by whatever had happened in the field.

She rose to her feet and appraised him. "Did you do this?" She waved her hand at Tommy's lifeless body.

"Yes, Mother." His eyes never left her face.

"Why?" Unfair as it might be, she needed to know if her son had killed his brother. Considering the heartless way Dema took Tommy's soul, she needed reassurance Elech wasn't more demon than human.

"There was a wolf. He was hunting a calf and..." Elech paused, turning to his brothers for reinforcement. "And I picked up the gun. I wanted to scare it away, but Tommy ran to chase it." He met her eyes once more. "I wanted Tommy to see that I could help. That I could do the job as well as he did." He ducked his head, shame written on his face.

*****

Days later Delia watched Elech from afar. Since the day they had buried Tommy, Elech had made a solitary pilgrimage to the edge of the family plot. After the third day, she followed him.

Today, the sun's rays streamed down like the heavens were opening their door to them. Her son dropped to his knees at the end of the grave and cried. Delila moved closer and strained to hear the words pouring from his mouth.

Dema materialized as if out of the very air she breathed and stood beside her.

"You know he looked up to that boy as his father?" His voice was dark. Haunted.

"Does that upset you?" She had had enough. How dare he stand there and patronize her? After everything between them, now he was jealous of Tommy? She fought the urge to scream and beat her hands against his unyielding chest.

"*I* am his father," he answered matter-of-factly.

"But you cannot be trusted with something as precious as my son." Delila met his cold dark stare with an accusatory one of her own. "You refused to spare my husband. You refused to spare my son, the person that your son idolized most. Yet, when I almost slipped into the ether, you did what?"

Dema grabbed her shoulders, turning her so that she had no choice but to look at him. "I risked *everything*." Each word was thick and solid, heavy with meaning.

Stunned into silence, Delila met the Devil's challenge with reverence.

"The fallen reserve just enough of their healing abilities to save themselves if injured on this plane," he paused, searching her eyes for something. "And I gave that up. For *you*."

Dema released her and continued. "For the woman who brought my son into the world. The woman I gave my heart to. The woman who betrayed my trust to save herself and refused to trust my ability to provide for her what was necessary."

He took a ragged breath, gathered his calm, and wiped the emotion from his face. "I gave up everything so that boy," he pointed a long finger at Elech, "would never know the heartache of losing you. The heartache of you hurting him the way you hurt me." Dema swallowed, shook his head, and retreated a few steps.

"Why?" Of all the questions flying through her head, it was the most important one to her.

Instead of answering, Dema leveled a dark look at her. "I won't make the same mistake again. Hug your sons tonight, witch, because by the time I finish with you, you will walk this plane alone. Not even our son will look upon you with love. That is a promise I intend to keep."

Delila's blood ran cold with his threats, but before she could respond, he was gone in the same way he appeared, silent, ominous, deadly.

Eight

HEARTACHE FOLLOWED DELILA like her shadow. In the time following her last encounter with Dema, life became much more dismal. Fredrick succumbed to disease, Eloise followed quickly thereafter. And day after day, month after month, Elech grew more distant.

She would often find him in the oddest of places talking to no one. The other children often commented on his strange behaviors, but Delila knew what was happening. Father and son had united. She could see the light and purity in Elech wan while darkness took root and grew rampant.

One summer day Delila overheard her daughters Calliope and Thea discussing the latest developments in their youngest brother.

"Did you see him with that man the other day?"

"Yes. How could I miss him? He's so..." Thea trailed off, a dreamy look on her face.

"Tall? Handsome? Mysterious?" Calliope offered.

"All of that and still so much more," Thea agreed. "Did you see the way he looked at us? He looked downright hungry. Starved, almost like we might be the meal he needed for survival."

Thea always had a flare for the dramatic. Her daughter stood at the threshold of maturity, and Delila wouldn't put it past Dema to notice. Delila rounded the corner and joined her giggling daughters in the sitting room.

"What is this I hear? Has a suitor come for you that I'm unaware of?" She took a seat beside Thea and picked up her darning basket.

"No, Mother," Thea answered.

"But Elech has a new friend who would be a lovely suitor," Calliope finished. "We should invite him to dinner. I think he's new in town. It would be nice to offer him some hospitality. Give him a place to hang his cloak and enjoy a hot meal."

"I hoped I had taught you better than that, Calliope. It isn't proper for a lady to invite a strange man into her home." She leveled a chastising look at her young daughters. "And I'd appreciate if you both concentrated more on the housework than the friends your brother surrounds himself with." She returned her basket to a spot near the fireplace and left them in silence. Elech was next on her list of children to rein in.

*****

She found him standing at the family plot. The small cemetery grew all too often these days. Three of her children lay here. Their souls at rest where they may be, and with each passing day Delila believed her time to join them drew closer.

"Mother." Clipped words was the fashion of the day with her son. "To what do we owe the pleasure?" Elech threw out his arms as if including all who rested in this hallowed place.

"I need to speak to you."

He chuckled, his laugh low and dark even though he was still young in years. "Mother, you are one lie followed by another. Why now do you think it important to talk?"

"I know you and Dema are speaking. Your sisters have seen you together."

"And what? Are you jealous?" A knowing sneer lit his young face. "Does knowing your lover walks this plane seeking another upset you, Mother?"

Rage boiled her blood. "That's quite enough, Elech," she seethed between clenched teeth. "Whatever he has said was meant to poison you. Let me tell you the truth." She took a deep breath. "Your real father is the love of my life. He made me come alive, gave light to the darkness, and showed me that true love was possible.

"But I was too young and scared to hand over all of me to him. I held fast to my sense of self-preservation and only turned over my heart. It was in my act of preservation that he feels I betrayed him; as I'm sure he's told you. What he doesn't know is that I loved him. My heart is still broken into shards from the night he let Thomas die, though."

Delila's lashes kissed her cheek as the sting of truth rolled through her. "I should have trusted your father to make things right, but instead I held onto my wounded pride and took matters into my own hands." Her head drooped with her shoulders.

"Your father let Thomas fade away because of jealousy that wasn't warranted. And now I hear that he is revealing himself plain enough that your sisters may set their sights upon him. I need this to end. Now." Her voice was more whisper than demand.

"You ask more than he will want to give. Mercy is no longer part of his agenda where you are concerned."

"Agenda?"

"You see Mother, you gave your heart to the devil. He used it for his own gains because you were the vessel he needed to ensure the delivery of me." Elech plucked a blade of grass from the ground and twirled it between his fingers. "Now, it is my turn to reveal a truth." He released the blade of grass from his grasp, but instead of falling to the earth, it hung suspended in the air twirling as if his fingers still manipulated it. A gasp left her mouth.

"Mere parlor tricks, Mother." Elech's face lightened for the first time in months and a rarely seen glint came to his eye. "You were chosen for a reason; like a prize bull needing a solid heifer to breed the strongest heir. You did your job well enough, as you can plainly see." A wicked smile creased his lips as the blade of grass burst into flames. "But now, you are useless to me, Mother..."

Delila's heart jumped into her throat, her lungs refused breath, and the world spun faster as her legs gave out. She awoke, much as she had years ago, on her kitchen floor. Dema's dark eyes peered into her soul and sent her reeling.

"Please, let me be," she pled.

"Witch, I could not leave you if heaven commanded it to be so." He cocked his head in question. "Why after all these years do you fear me?"

"I know the truth. Your son," she tossed her head side to side looking for the son in question but found nothing. "Your son explained my part in your plan."

"Pray tell, what part is that?"

"The part of the whore." Shame coated her words and lingered on her skin.

"You were never my whore, witch. You were his," Dema's voice dropped an octave and wrapped around her with a familiarity that Delila had long forgotten. "Until you understand that, this rift between us will exist." Dema placed a finger under her chin and tilted her lips up to meet his.

Feather light kisses graced her face, lips, and neck, warming her tortured soul.

"I don't understand," she protested. The war

between love and hate raged within her.

"Mere mortals cannot," he stated simply, and in the next instant he was gone.

Nine

"HOW DARE YOU?" Elech seethed.

"How dare *you*?" Demogorgon countered. "I have given you the key to greatness and you squander it to hurt the woman you owe your life to?" He snaked a hand around his son's throat and applied enough pressure to remind his son whom it was he challenged.

"She betrayed us," Elech whined. He squirmed in his father's grasp.

"No. She betrayed me. Not you." He released his grip and paced the field that was once fertile with life, but was now barren and lifeless, just as he felt. "Drammelech, your mother is a very powerful witch. It is in both of our interests to not cause her distress. Unless, of course, you wish to be banned to the Underworld beside me."

"She cannot do that." Panic painted his son's face.

"You underestimate her, my son." Demogorgon nodded. "Indeed she has the power to do exactly that."

"No. She is not like us. She's weak. Fragile. Human." Elech sneered.

"You have so much to learn, and I fear I won't have the chance to teach you. Your mother is so much more than you can imagine. I waited a millennium for a witch of her strength and fortitude to come along so that you could be conceived." Memories washed over Demogorgon in a torrent.

There had been many witches before her. All with their own appeal, but none who came so openly and willingly to him. None who had seen beyond what his presence meant. None of them had loved him without condition or restraint, or had looked upon him as a man; a man who wasn't fallen and who wasn't tainted by one dark mark on his soul. A man she could love.

Demogorgon closed his eyes against the onslaught the visions created. How he had cut down his onetime friend, Nephilim, for the chance to own a love that would never be his. That vision was quickly followed by another. This time, the figure of Annika, the woman who had tricked him into furthering her vendetta, flashed before his eyes. Beauty and false pretense had tricked him into thinking she wanted to be his. But alas, all Annika had wanted was their fall. His fall from grace, and her banishment to this plane. Their falling and the revelation that she had never seen him as anything more than a means to changing her station still stung. Ultimately, he had learned that being the supreme leader of all witches was no longer to her liking and he believed she would soon be up to her ancient tricks.

Of course, his being charged as the ruler of the Underworld had been an unexpected twist in Annika's plan. Although, it was a station he only had hope to leave with the birth of an heir that could walk between the planes and plead his case before the Sovereign Court. While Demogorgon searched the earth for a witch to give him an heir, Annika wasted her days trying to devise the spell that would open all the planes to her once again.

Drammelech sat poised on the precipice of greatness. One his son could only imagine, but not grasp unless he lost the bitterness that clung to him. Demogorgon accepted his role in that. After Delila betrayed and banished him, he had spent his days plotting his return, revenge, and retribution. And the moment a weak-willed witch called him to surface and condemned her soul to his keeping, he had gone right to his son. In his anger, Demogorgon had colored his every word with spite, hatred, and worst of all, jealousy. That was until he began to watch Delila.

She had struggled to keep her wits about her on a good day. It had seemed her heart was in tatters. At first Demogorgon believed she still mourned the loss of that fool, Thomas, but one night of watching her sleep cured him of that notion. Under the spell of the moon and slumber, she had caressed her skin with his name; a sigh on her lips. The stain of color on her porcelain skin pounded new life in his heart. After that night, he kept a close watch on her, seeing the love she had once promised to him never far from the surface.

It was her love that compelled him to save her. The day she learned he was walking side by side with his son had been too much for her bruised heart just as the ground had been too hard for her fragile skull. But when Delila's soul had clamored to split from her body Demogorgon had acted on pure instinct. He wept over her, healing her earthen body, and tied her soul to his. Forever. One day, she might hate him for his actions, but with eternity before them, Demogorgon held onto the hope that he would make her understand.

A metallic click transported him back to the field. Standing before him, Drammelech held a gun at his shoulder, aimed at Demogorgon's chest.

"Your heart weakens you, Father."

"And your impatience will be your undoing." Demogorgon shook his head and retreated to the Underworld.

*****

From his throne in what humans called 'Hell', Demogorgon watched his son on the viewing orb. Drammelech was hungry for power, a power that would undo him if he wasn't careful. It was from that very spot Demogorgon witnessed what would define his son's path in life. He watched as one by one his son's brothers fell.

One dropped with the speed of a well-aimed bullet. Another screamed as flames licked at his heels and roasted him alive. Several days later a sister was lost during childbirth, and another still was taken down by a horse. At each graveside memorial, Demogorgon stood hidden beside Delila. He could feel the accusation that arced through her thoughts. She blamed him for each loss, and it built within her until she feared for Elech's life as well.

Demogorgon sat invisible beside her at night as she begged her witch ancestors to give her a sign to stop the reign of terror, the terror she assumed was at his command. She no longer sighed his name in her sleep. Instead, she shrieked and cried, her body shaking.

His son was right. She was his weakness. She was what could cut him down to his knees, rip his wings from his back, and be the end of him. Because of her, he would be imprisoned by his love and ended.

Cut down.

Defeated.

And all hell would reign on earth because he no longer had the power to do what was necessary to put a stop to his son's madness.

Ten

ON THE EVE of Elech's fifteenth birthday, despite this day being full of light and gaiety, darkness settled the way it did every night. Flora and Gwendolyn were now safely in the homes of their new husbands; a pair of brothers who had somehow managed to stay unmarried until they were well into their twenties.

The relief she felt was short-lived. A knock on her bedroom door sounded and there he stood, tall and brooding in her doorway.

"Yes, Elech?"

"You looked relieved today, Mother. Getting my sisters married off will not protect them. Father will find them and strike them down in good time. I'm afraid," Elech lamented.

"My son, as long as he views your siblings as a threat, he will continue to wreak havoc in our lives." She laid her head on the bed and wished for sleep to come.

"Mother, you deserve better than he can offer you. He haunts us in the hope that you will create the pathway to the Overworld for him."

"The Overworld?" Her attention snapped back to Elech, eyes wide with awareness. Years ago Dema had mentioned something of the like, but she had thought her involvement in his gaining access to the Overworld ended with the birth of their child.

"Didn't you know? He speaks often of the prophecy." Elech sat beside her on the bed and patted her arm, pity in his touch. "To regain access to the Overworld, he must first find a witch who could," he raised a finger and ticked them off as he spoke. "See the inherent good in him, give him an heir, and upon her death plead on his behalf to the Sovereign Court."

He dropped his hand and stood. "As I count it, he already has two of those, all he needs is to drive you into the grave. Disposing of your human heirs allows him the extra power required to bend your will to his service."

A gasp ripped from her lips. Of course Dema would use her children to further his agenda. He had used Thomas's death in much the same way. Her brain began to boil over with thoughts of spells that would save them all from Dema's scheme.

"But there are tales of a dagger that will end him, Mother, and I will search for it until the end of time to protect you." With a shrug of his shoulders Elech left her alone.

*****

The next morning Delila woke to banging on her door. Outside stood a lawman with a firearm gripped in his hand.

"Mrs. Dewsberry?"

"Yes," she answered.

"Will you invite me in to your home?" The question hit her ears like a command.

"What is going on, sir?" She retreated from the doorway and allowed him access to her home.

"There has been a disturbing accusation," he answered as his gaze travelled the length of her.

Her breakfast threatened to come back from its current placement deep in her stomach. "What kind of accusation?"

"Witchcraft."

That was all Delila needed to hear. Her worst fears were coming true, but how? She had instructed her daughters in the ways of their ancestors and she had been very careful to keep her craft a secret. It had been necessary to armor her daughters against Dema, and any potential harm he might bring, but they knew they could not make mention of their ancestors nor their magic. Delila knew they would never tell a soul their secret. She fell back into a chair in the sitting room, shock beating against her.

"Are you aware that your daughter's believe they belong to a coven of witches?" The lawman asked.

"A coven? Witches?" She shook her head. "I don't understand. I've raised them right. We attend the church in town, and we pray to God above." She met the stranger's eyes. "Who has made this claim against them?"

"Someone saw them dancing in the moonlight last night."

"They were married yesterday. I'm sure they were celebrating their new lives," she offered as her mind raced to find reasonable explanations that would save her daughters.

"It was their husbands that found them," he continued. "They were in the buff and dancing with what appeared to be the devil."

No. No, no, no. This could not be happening. Dema had corrupted her daughters and now they would burn for it. How dare he?

The man sidestepped past her, motioned for her to wait while he went room-to-room. She could hear him rifling through her belongings, but stayed statue still. When he found nothing of consequence, he returned to her. "It's only because they have admitted to falling for the devil's charms of their own free will that you, and the rest of your family, are not being charged as well."

"What's going on in here?" Elech's voice carried over to them as he stomped his feet at the kitchen door.

"I was just telling Mrs. Dewsberry that her daughters have been convicted as witches." The lawman eyed Elech. "You wouldn't happen to know anything about that, would you?"

"What? That's preposterous." Elech narrowed his eyes and leveled a hard stare at the man. Delila could feel her son's power brimming under the weight of it.

"Which of my sisters have been convicted?"

"One Flora McDowell and one Gwendolyn McDowell."

"With what proof?" Elech challenged.

"They were seen dancing with the devil," Delila whispered, cutting her eyes to her son.

"I find it convenient that this has come to light before the McDowell family pays the dual dowries due for the marriages of their sons to my sisters," Elech growled. "How can we prove they aren't witches?"

"They've already confessed, sir," the man retorted, a flicker of glee dancing in his eyes.

"And what, pray tell, did you do to them to get this confession?" Elech pulled himself up to his full height, towered over the man, and stepped close.

"That is none of your concern." The lawman stepped back and marched through the door he had entered. "If you want to say goodbye, come to the town square this night at sundown."

With the slam of the door Delila crumpled to the floor.

"Mother?" Elech knelt beside her and grabbed her hands in his. "I'm sure father was not to blame for this. He wouldn't be careless."

"You, yourself, said he was out to end my line. Why wouldn't he go to the girls and make sure to seduce them with witnesses?"

"Mother, those men have stayed unmarried far too long for me to believe that this isn't a coincidence. I'd wager they are trying to get out of paying the dowry."

Delila wanted to believe his words, but there was too much at stake for her remaining children. "We will never speak of this again. Do you understand?"

"But we have to go to them. We need to know if this was the work of *him*." Bitterness hung off his words.

"No! We cannot go anywhere near there or we will be added to the fire for being sympathizers. I forbid you from leaving this house tonight." She rose to her feet, gathered her strength, and walked away from the last person who she wanted to trust to keep them all alive. "And I forbid you from breathing a word of this to anyone."

As she left the room Delila heard something even more disturbing than the news of her daughters impending deaths; Elech's quiet laughter. Her blood froze in her veins. What had she done? And then the truth hit her with the force of a ton of stones landing on her chest.

She had created a monster.

ELEVEN

DEMOGORGON FLICKED THE dual tips of his tongue against his upper lip as he sat transfixed on the images playing before his eyes. Two more of Delila's children were about to be sacrificed to appease their greedy son. And here he sat, unable to do anything about it.

In Demogorgon's last jaunt to the surface, Elech had again threatened him, this time with a long bladed knife inscribed with his angelic name. A spelled instrument of that caliber would be the end of him for sure, but it was even more fitting that his son embodied the evil that humans equated with the devil.

But unless Elech went after Delila, Demogorgon would stay put on his throne in Hell. Risking his life to intervene would only cause more pain, because if he died before Delila, her soul would wander the Underworld alone until another fallen king was assigned thanks to the "out" in his banishment. Simply put, if ever during his time at his post he showed growth befitting the risen, he again would be welcomed into the Overworld upon his demise. Looking back on it now, it occurred to him that the moment he sacrificed his tears for Delila, he had gained reentry rights.

With a swipe of his arm, the scene on the orb before him fluttered until it refocused on a large piling of kindling. The sun and moon went to war over the town square as if there was a winner to be proclaimed, and in time, the darkness found victory. He focused his eyes on the two golden haired beauties huddled together, their bodies trembling.

It never stopped amazing him how very similar all of Delila's daughters looked. They all shared the same sun-kissed hair, porcelain skin, light eyes, and rose-colored cheeks. It was as if each daughter were a reincarnation of Delila, right down to the tiny bump on their collective noses.

Their fear tore at his heart, each sniffle, each sob, each dry heave. His heart broke over and over again while the last moments of their lives stretched out. With a wave of his hand over the orb, he could see the farm he had grown to love. With little thought for his safety, he made a decision that had the potential to be his undoing and donned his cloak. In an instant he stood in the cell before the girls, a solemn expression set on his face.

"Don't fear, I've been sent for you."

The shorter of the girl's tears flowed fast while the other regarded him with wary eyes. "Are you an angel?" She uttered beneath her breath and rubbed her eyes.

"Once." His answer was plain. "But tonight I

will be what stands between you and an eternity of pain until your soul lets go."

"Why?" Disbelief colored her question as her sister moaned like a wounded animal.

"I owe your mother." A simple answer to a complicated question. "Just know that you will not be alone tonight." He slid the hood of the cloak over his head and melted from their view, but he stayed close in case they needed reassurance. If all went as he expected, Delila and the rest of her family would stay safely tucked away at the farm this night. He hoped that would be the case.

He listened as the women spoke among themselves, crying and questioning what had happened. From the little he could discern, they both recalled falling asleep beside their new husbands. And yet, they seemingly shared a dream where music enticed them to dance. Neither woman could remember the other in their dream state, let alone the devil, but given that a man had both materialized and vanished in front of them just moments ago, there was plenty of room for confusion.

Together, the young women discussed an attempt to weave a spell to escape their prison bars, but when it occurred to them that their mother and remaining siblings would be charged next, the idea was quickly tossed aside.

"Mother warned us against using the craft," the taller one reminded.

"Yes, but would she sit here and await her death knowing that she had the power to stop it?"

"Flora, you know she would go to the ends of the world to save us from this if she could." The woman put her arms around her sister and hugged her tight. "We won't be alone tonight. That man promised. He said that mother sent him," she reminded.

"Gwendolyn," Flora dropped her voice to a low whisper and Demogorgon moved closer to hear her words. "Is it possible that the man mother sent to save us is the devil?"

"Hush, child," Gwendolyn scolded. "You must never utter those words. Never. Even as the fire eats at your flesh, you must never call the devil's name." She grabbed Flora's shoulders and shook her. "Do you understand me? Even if that man is the devil you must not let anyone know that he is present. If you do, mother and the rest of them will be next."

Flora squirmed under the pressure of her sister's fingers digging into her skin. "I promise," she winced.

"Good, now hold my hands. The sun has set and it will soon be time. I don't want to waste any more of our last moments upset. I'll lend you my strength and you lend me yours. Together we will walk into the afterlife hand in hand." She nodded her head. "Together always."

"Together always," Flora echoed, her voice wavering.

*****

Demogorgon stood by as their jailers dragged them

from the cell and tied them to the stakes high upon a pile of dry, split wood. He watched as tears flowed silently down their beautiful faces, and their hands struggled to clasp one another behind their backs. Moving was too trite of a word for the scene that unfolded before him. Heartbreaking was more fitting.

When a man who appeared to be in charge approached with a flaming torch, Demogorgon stepped forward. Unseen, he walked right past the man and up the woodpile. With a touch of magic, he allowed his voice to travel to the sisters' ears.

"I'm here young ones. Trust in me that no pain will come to you. Fear will make you want to cry out, but be strong. For once the flames close in, I will guide your souls from your bodies. You will feel no pain. No burning. No nothing. Before long, an angel will come and guide you to the other side. Do you trust me?" He stepped back and waited.

"We trust you," the one named Gwendolyn whispered.

"Good."

It was a matter of moments before flames ran up the wood, crackling, sparking, eating it alive, but the women stood fast. Their brave faces met the rising smoke and loud jeers from the crowd. True to his word, Demogorgon reached his hands into their bodies and yanked their souls free before the fire could touch their skin. There would be consequences for his actions doled out upon his demise, but as with all else in his existence, he would endure them. For he was the one who brought the evil to life that caused this needless suffering.

He felt a warm light on his wings while he and the souls waited outside of town. "It's time for you to move on," he spoke to the souls, who still even in this spiritual form clutched one another's hands.

"Thank you," chorused around him as their spirits echoed off the night.

He turned from them, ready to retreat to his place in the Underworld, when a flutter of heavy wings sounded above him.

"Demogorgon the Despotic, I see you are again at your old tricks."

"Brother Nephilim, you give me credit where none is due." Demogorgon spread his wings and braced for what was sure to come. The sound of an arrow being run across the string of a bow scratched his ears.

"Please, sir," one of the women spoke. "This man has been so kind as to save us from the pain and suffering of the fire."

Demogorgon looked back at the women and gave them the hint of a smile before he disappeared just in time for the arrow to pierce the air where he had been standing.

Twelve

THAT NIGHT AS she imagined a blazing fire ending the lives of her daughters, Delila ransacked the room searching for her journal. She cracked the spine on the leather bound tome to reach the middle pages and hoped they stayed intact. It was her almost completed book, save these pages mid-way through. She had left them blank on a whim one day after communing with her ancestors without a clear understanding as to why she had left them blank, but now it all became clear.

She needed to make sure this spell would be buried amongst other innocuous entries for the year so that no one would think any further about it and inadvertently allow her son access to the Overworld.

She added ingredient after ingredient to the simmering pot hanging over the hearth. In went sage, rosewater, and a lock of Elech's hair saved from when he was an infant. Then she added the blood infused rose thorn. It had been hard to come by, but without it she worried the spell wouldn't hold. As the mixture boiled, her mind raced. So much had happened. So much regret plagued her. Tears that had threatened to flow for days now streamed freely down her face.

Of all her children, she hated to do this to Elech. From the moment of his conception, she had known he was the first of her children to be conceived with love in her heart, and yet, the influence of his father was what would be his undoing. Without her to stop him, he would be able to do what Dema was as of yet unable to do. He would rule the people of this plane with heartless abandon.

As it was, Dema had done all he could to take the liberty of controlling her life. Slowly but surely disposing of her other children and ensuring she would live to see each of their tragic deaths.

No matter how much love she offered Elech, his father had wormed into the boy's soul and offered the promise of greatness. A greatness that she had fought to keep from corrupting her only remaining son. Her tears landed with a sizzle in the steaming pot and added the most essential ingredient - her heartbreak.

It was done without fanfare or any of the usual joy that swelled in her heart at the completion of a spell of this magnitude. Instead, her heart hung empty in her chest and beat a slow, steady pulse that reminded her of her footsteps that had accompanied each of her deceased children to their final resting places. Out of thirteen children brought into this world, only four remained, and one was the son of the devil himself.

Before extinguishing the flame beneath the pot, one last thought occurred to her. Her heirs would need protection from the wrath that would surely result from her actions today. She selected four slices of smoky quartz from her jewel box and dropped them into the bubbling mixture. Before the next day was done, she'd use her tools to engrave and seal them with silver. It would give her great pleasure to hang the pendants with ribbon on the necks of her remaining daughters.

With these, they would be safe from the prying eyes of the devil. She would have to find a way to impress upon them the urgency to wear the pendants at all times without scaring them. However, she wasn't sure if there was any way to convince her stubborn daughters without shining the light of truth on the reality of their brother's origin. Even if it was an origin she thought Thea and Calliope might know after having seen Dema and Elech together. But if it ensured their safety, she would do it. She would tell them her secrets if it meant protecting them from the terror she had forced into their lives.

She drew a wooden spoon through the thickening liquid in the pattern of the pentagram. It was a spiritual symbol of her people and would add ancestral power to her spell. She repeated the motion twelve more times for good measure then put out the flame.

In the time it took for the liquid to cool, she had readied the tools. Each felt heavy in her small hands. All the time she'd spent in her shop would finally come in handy and result in something more meaningful than a token of beauty to wear.

She reached into the pot and removed the four pieces of stone. Each was warm in her hand and smooth to the touch. They would be perfect stones for the pendants.

She labored all night until each stone was sealed with an ouroboros, and the pentagram had been painstakingly etched into the surface of the hard rock. She pawed through the remnants of her darning bin until she came upon enough lengths of ribbon to hang the pendants from.

Once the sun rose, she would make the trek into town to see Esther and there she would wrap the ribbon around her neck personally. It was what must be done. A light knock at the door called her from her work. On the other side stood Thea. Her face wrinkled when the smell of the long-cooled potion assaulted her nose.

"Mother, you never came to bed last night. I thought the worst might have befallen you."

Delila went to her daughter and enveloped her in an embrace that was meant to express what mere words could not. It wasn't until Thea wiggled from her clasp with questioning eyes that Delila realized tears she had been holding back since finishing the pendants had broken free.

"Mother! What's wrong?" Thea wiped at the tears on Delila's face with the pads of her fingers.

"Dear child, I need you to make me a promise."

"You're scaring me, Mother." Matching wetness clung to her daughter's lashes.

"I know, but it can't be helped." She took one of the pendants from the table where she'd been working all night and tied it around Thea's neck. "You must promise to never take this off. Not until you have a daughter of your own. Then you must pass it along to her. Do you understand?"

"No. Please Mother, explain what is happening." Thea fingered the pendant hanging between her breasts. "I don't understand what is happening."

"Sweet child, I need you to trust me. Your brother isn't what you think. He will need to be stopped, but I know I will never be able to destroy him myself. It will be left to our descendants. However, they will need something that ties them to me to harness our ancestral power."

"The power we can't even lay claim to without fear of hanging or burning?" Accusation replaced the sadness in Thea's eyes. "I have no intention of thrusting that upon my children, Mother. You know how I feel about that, about what has happened to..." The words stuck in her throat. "Know that I will pass this along as you wish, but I will never tell my kin that they can access our ancestral right. Never."

"Thea." The plea ripped from her soul.

"No Mother. Never. Ask me anything else, but that I cannot promise you." With that, Thea walked out of the room and didn't look back.

Not even once.

*****

Even with her brisk pace, the journey into town took longer than Delila thought was possible. When she arrived at Esther's home she was met by the one person she least expected. Elech leaned against the front wall of the modest home, a wry smile on his face.

"You're too late Mother." His eyes glowered beneath his long dark lashes. "I suppose I should've told you that I had the ability to track my siblings, but it had been one more thing in the long list that made me different. And an interesting thing occurred today; quirky little Thea vanished from my radar. At first I thought it might have been the work of father, but when I arrived here Esther told me that I must be mad. Imagine that Mother. Me mad?" A low laugh rumbled from his chest.

"Elech, whatever are you talking about?" Dread ripped at Delila leaving her unable to make sense of his words. "Please explain what brings you to Esther's." She feigned confusion as her mind raced.

"Don't patronize me," he spat. "I know why you are here. You will not banish me into the Underworld with *him*." He glared behind her with enough venom, that she turned, expecting to see Dema.

"Elech, I don't know what he has said to you, but I would never betray you like that." A lump rose in her throat as her deceit washed her from head to toe. "I'm just here to visit your sister."

Her son shook his head as if to ward off her lies. "Oh Mother, we both know you are here to verify that she is alive and well. Very much like I expect

Thea to be, although I no longer can connect with her."

He arched his back and lifted himself to his full height. At slightly over six foot her son had grown into an impressive presence, far surpassing the typical growth rate of her human children. She watched his every move with great care. For even though she loved her son, he was as tainted by evil as any could be. Her heart sank in her chest and the lump in her throat bobbed. Without Dema around to confront, it occurred to her that this time her son might be the cause for concern.

"What have you done, Elech?"

"Don't worry, Mother. It's nothing that dark magic couldn't reverse." The smile on his face morphed into the smirk that reminded her of Dema. Darkness lived in that look. "But, be certain that you cannot stop what has been put into motion. I'll have taken care of Calliope and Thea before you can gather enough strength to fight me." He leaned down and placed a chaste kiss on the top of her head then slid past her and strode off into the darkness.

Fight me? Realization made her shudder. This had been Elech's work. His and his alone, and now he had promised the same fate for Calliope and Thea.

Delila gathered her wits about her and rapped on the door. Esther's husband, Alexander, opened it, his tear-stained face saying more than any words could. With her breath lodged in her lungs she pushed her way past him and into her daughter's home. Esther was laid out in the front room, lifeless and pale. Someone placed a hand on her shoulder, but nothing could comfort the pain that ran rampant through her veins.

Elech had done this. She was certain of it now. Elech had probably been to blame for the deaths of all her children. And maybe even her own brief brush with the endless slumber. Somehow Elech had known that she had worked against him and he'd gone and taken his revenge on the people she loved. Without speaking a word to Alexander, Delila left, knowing she would find a similar scene at Calliope's home.

All because the tangible evidence that remained from her transgression with Dema was hungry. Hungry for power and control. His actions were enough to solidify in her heart what needed to be done.

Delila never looked back at Ester's house. Instead she fastened one of the remaining three amulets around her neck and for the first time since Elech was born, walked with the knowledge that nothing would be able to hurt her. Not her lies, her betrayals, her heart. Nothing.

The trek down the dirt path that led to the farmhouse was eerily quiet. In the distance she could hear the animalistic shriek of what she instinctively knew to be her son. Her pace never stumbled, nor did it quicken. Instead she walked with the cool confidence of a woman ahead of her time. She held the power to change the future. This she was certain of more than anything else. She made her way right into the back room of the barn where her materials still littered the workspace.

Delila relit the fire and began pulling vials off the shelves. Into the pot went a bit of this, and a dash of that, and a final pinch of something else. She coded the ingredients in her journal for future reference and stripped out of her frock.

When the liquid began to smoke, and the first bubble of a boil rose to the surface, she removed her concoction from the fire and set it aside to cool. Once she could stand the temperature of the liquid, Delila immersed her hand into the pot and began the ritual of sliding the salve over every inch of her exposed skin. When she was as covered as the reach of her arms allowed she walked into the moonlit night. With her hands thrust outward, Delila lifted her face to the heavens and recited the spell that had banished her lover from this world.

Although, this time the spell was amplified by the salve, the moon, and the pendant she wore. It would seal Dema in the Underworld and hold Elech to this plane until a direct descendant of her family line undid the spell. She added another verse to the spell in hopes that it would tighten the veil on Elech further and protect the humans from his war cry for power. The cries from the darkness grew into howls; painful, hatred-filled howls that pierced the air.

She felt Elech banging against the border that surrounded her and his childhood home. Good. Her spell would hold. That was the benefit of her lineage. She walked toward the small lake on the property and didn't stop until the soft floor of it no longer met her toes.

Delila ducked beneath the surface and willed the water to wash away the memory of Dema. If she would ever be able to complete the next part of her spell, she needed to forget every happy moment. Passion, love, adoration; they all needed to be erased. Her heart began to crumble in her chest as her magic tugged at the interwoven memories that made up a lifetime of yearning, desire, love. Emptiness slowly replaced them as her lungs began to fight the lack of fresh breath. Her feet kicked toward the surface, but her arms worked against it.

The duality warred with her body, mind, and spirit. She needed to undo everything that had called Elech into being. If that meant losing her life? Then that's what she would give. She would give up the right to breathe if it would keep him from gaining access to his father, or worse-yet, the innocent souls in the Overworld who would be ill equipped to protect themselves from the likes of him. If only she had the willpower to banish her son as well, but that she could not do. Even now, knowing what she did, she couldn't allow for that much suffering.

It had been her own selfish desires that had cost them so much, and if she had to pay with her already cursed soul to keep them safe, she would. She'd pay that price a thousand times over so the Overworld could stay safely locked away.

A flash of color exploded behind the cover of her eyelids as her brain began to misfire. Her feet thrashed against the force of her arms struggling to hold her beneath the surface. Somewhere, deep inside, she knew she was dying. She knew this moment would be her undoing.

The memory of Dema's lips on hers was ever-present in the recesses of her mind. She couldn't erase them and therefore couldn't complete the spell without cursing her body to the Underworld. In death, she prayed that the memories of him would be unable to follow. As the thought crossed her mind, her feet stilled, her arms went limp, and her lungs finally took the water-filled breath they had been longing for.

*****

The visage of death came for her. That's how he appeared, an angel of mercy shrouded in a cloak of death, not unlike Dema's. He ripped her soul from her body with pointed teeth, and dragged her into what she expected would be the fiery pits of Hell. And that's when it happened. Her soul, still clenched in the demon's teeth, bounced off some invisible barrier. He released her soul and struck out on his own. Again, he was turned away. He hissed and growled at her as the damage of her spell sank in. They were stuck on this plane.

"The king will not be happy." He spoke in the tongue of a foreign language, and yet she somehow knew his words. "He had fought to protect you all this time, from the spawn of your seed that brought about nothing but death and destruction, and now you've clipped his wings. For this, there will be hell to pay."

Thirteen

ELECH FELT THE moment his mother died. She had disappeared from his perception hours before, likely in the same manner that Thea had, but a splintering in his heart was all it took to be assured that the one woman he had loved above all others was gone from this plane.

His animal cries waned and human tears took their place. He crumpled to the ground in a heap of disarray. He tuned in to the pathway in his brain that allowed him access to his father and found it equally empty. Damn her. She had cut him off from everything.

He had always known she hadn't loved him as she had her other children, but this was all the proof he needed. Whatever had been her undoing, he was grateful for it. The woman didn't deserve to live in a world she held hostage from her son.

Under the night sky, he shifted his being into the shape of his father's origins; full man stature with the feather covered leathery wings like a bat and the long tail of a serpent. He spread his wings and took to the sky. The current of air rushing around his skin made him feel alive.

His father had warned him at a very young age that there was a chance his mother would betray him this way. She would lock him out of his rightful home and tie him to the Earth, but in doing so, she would open the door for him to access the powers that lay innate inside his being. Powers gifted by his father upon his birth, yet untouchable until the death of his human mother.

Now all he had to do was bide his time until the right woman came along to bear him an heir. A female heir would grant him the ability to break whatever magic his mother had put into place. He circled the nearest town until he found what he was looking for; a farm that sat outside of the town limits with light burning in a window.

If he had his father's luck, the answer to his problems would be wiggling in his arms in less than a year's time. He landed on the ground with a soft thud and embraced his human form. As the transition overtook him, pain flooded his system. Turning back to his full human form was like being stabbed by irons heated in Hell's fires. Had he known the pains he'd be forced to endure in the process of the transition back to human, he would've thought twice before taking to the air. When he could take no more, he fell to the ground and cried out. His mouth ached and the skin on his back where his wings had disappeared now burned, feeling split and tender in the breeze.

"Sir?" The gentle voice bounced around in his head at levels louder than he had ever before experienced. He forced his eyes upward and connected with the biggest eyes on the smallest face. So out of proportion was the woman standing at his side that he almost forgot the agony swelling inside him.

She looked young and innocent with fair skin and dark locks. There was something about her that offered him a reason to hope. Maybe it was her fearlessness in the face of a naked howling man in her yard in the middle of the night, or maybe it was the curious way her eyes traveled his body. Whatever it was, he threw all his focus into her and slowly stumbled to his feet. When he staggered she reached out to ease his fall.

The warmth of her touch sent shockwaves through his hypersensitive skin. A memory he thought long gone flashed in his mind's eye. He'd heard from his older brothers that no one was aware of the world at the moment of conception, regardless of his claims. He had forced the memories of his parents tangled together in sweat-slicked embraces to the far reaches of his memory. The passion and joy of their union, following like a clap of thunder chases a bolt of lightning.

Immediately he wanted those memories of his own making. He needed them, his body primed and ready. This young woman would do nicely.

Instinct drove his actions as he embraced her in arms that were now fully human once again. She didn't protest, nor squirm, when he lowered his lips to hers. Instead her warm rosebuds parted for him allowing him into the warmth of her oversized lips.

It wasn't until his tongue slipped into the recesses of her mouth that he noticed the difference. He pulled back and gently tapped his index finger to the tip, no, tips, of his tongue. His tongue was spilt like that of a snake. It must've happened during his transformation, but unlike the wings and tail it hadn't disappeared.

The woman gave him a tentative smile, added a single finger to the tips of his tongue, and giggled. He arranged his mouth into a matching grin and pulled her in close. Before long, he would be ripping down the magical walls his mother had hastily built.

It would be his legacy on every plane. His father would again wish to have him at his side, and he would be revered, as he should be. With this simple human woman, he would forever change the world. It was that thought that took root in his mind as he tore her clothes from her body and sank into her depths.

Passion wasn't his focus; survival was. He lost himself in the moment and came to in a tangle of limbs, slicked with blood. Not his blood. He was certain of that. Instead he met the eyes of the woman beneath him. Eyes that were slowly losing their luster. He watched as her skin greyed and her veins turned black as if venom flowed through them. A final breath of air escaped her lips and her body went limp.

Elech's blood ran cold and he bolted into the darkness without a care. He needed a new plan; a plan that would grant him his rightful place in history.

Under the cover of darkness, Elech skittered from place to place until he finally settled in a small shack among the wooded pines. It was here he would uncover the key to his success with nothing more than time and patience.

WANT MORE?

WANT A SNEAK peek at what's coming next for Elech? Check out Jeni's website at www.jeniburns.com for a sneak peek of *Sacrificed*, Twisted Fate Novella #2 and *Revealed*, Twisted Fated Novella #3. Both will be released in May 2015.

BIOGRAPHY

JENI BURNS is a Jersey girl living in a southern world. While she's firmly planted in the South with her husband, two kids, and one massive poodle, her heart still lives in the Northwestern part of New Jersey where her characters reside. Since writing about home is cheaper than airfare, she spends much of her time living vicariously in NJ's snowy winters and humidity-free summers.

Jeni has been telling stories since she first learned how to string two words together. Thanks to her mom and her middle school English teacher both telling her she should be a writer, she now happily spends her days writing all the stories that continuously float around in her head while drinking fabulous decaf coffees.

Made in the USA
Middletown, DE
21 March 2017